NIGHT BEFORE
CHRISTMAS
IN COLORADO

Sue Carabine

Illustrations by

Shauna Mooney Kawasaki

GIBBS·SMITH
PUBLISHER

SALT LAKE CITY

05 04 03 02 01 00   6 5 4 3 2 1

Copyright © 2000 by Gibbs Smith, Publisher

Published by
Gibbs Smith, Publisher
P.O. Box 667
Layton, Utah 84041

Orders: (1-800) 748-5439
E-mail: *info@gibbs-smith.com*
Website: *www.gibbs-smith.com*

Designed and produced by
   Mary Ellen Thompson, TTA Design
Printed in Hong Kong

ISBN 0-87905-997-4

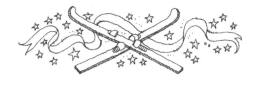

'Twas the night before Christmas
a short while ago
In the snow-beautiful state
of Colorado.

The kids were brimming
with anticipation,
Their folks concentrating
on Yule decorations!

They knew that St. Nicholas
was packing his gear,
For he and his reindeer
would soon arrive here.

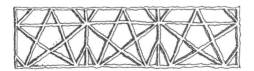

This state had to be
his most favorite place
'Cause Christmas is visible
in each little space.

But at the North Pole
in Nick's snug little den,
He sat down and read
these words over again:

"Dear Santa," Tom wrote,
"I feel very sad.
And when I see pictures
of you, I get mad!

"I love Christmas so much
and, Santa, you too,
But lately I've wondered
if it is all true.

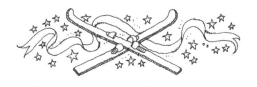

"Do you really make toys
in a land filled with snow
That's cold, white, and fluffy?
I'm dying to know!

"This place where I live
is so sunny and warm,
I've never seen what you
would call a 'snowstorm.'

"So please, dear old Santa,
help me to believe
That you're real and it's you
who brings gifts Christmas Eve."

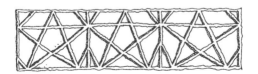

St. Nicholas just sat there
and shook his white head,
"Someone should help
little Tommy," he said.

Then all of a sudden
he jumped from his chair,
"We'll head for the Rockies,
there's lots of snow there!

"I'll take young Tom with me,
together we'll go
To this side of heaven—
to Colorado!"

With that, Santa kissed
Mrs. Claus on the cheek,
Said, "This shouldn't take
much more than a week."

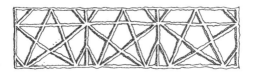

Of course Mrs. Claus
caught the gleam in his eye,
Said softly, "I'll see you
tomorrow, dear. 'Bye!"

She knew that her Nick
loved this part of the world
And would play in the snow
till his eyelashes curled!

So that's how it was,
and in no time at all,
Santa flew with young Tommy,
his reindeer, and haul.

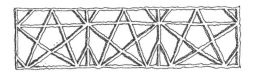

They checked into Pike's Peak
at Nick's workshop there,
Collected the toys that were
made with such care.

Tom's eyes opened wide
and before it got dark
He stared at the wonders
of quaint Estes Park.

Snow glistened and sparkled
on mountains so high.
"I should never have doubted
dear Santa," he sighed.

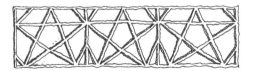

The sleigh landed softly
on each family's roof;
Nick left gifts each time
that were more than enough.

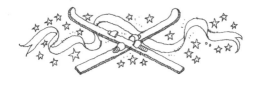

Tom spied the bridge spanning
a canyon named Gore,
Saw great Mesa Verde,
and still wanted more!

In old Steamboat Springs,
Tom swore he could see
Some fun-loving cowboys
out on a wild spree!

Then things got exciting
when he heard St. Nick call,
"I feel energetic.
Let's go play football!"

They flew on to Denver
to find the Mile High—
A stadium, that is—
Tom couldn't think why!

He found out quite soon
when Nick pulled up his sleigh
And jumped on the field
most determined to play!

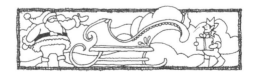

He supported the Broncos,
knew he could help out,
Brought Elway back home
'cause he carried some clout.

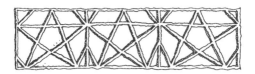

St. Nick caught John's pass
and, while juggling the ball,
Belly shaking with laughter,
he tried not to fall!

Then just as a fan called,
"Hey, who's that clown?"
He rushed the defense
and made a touchdown!

The Broncs cheered Nick on
as he flew up and away;
There were many fun places
to visit that day:

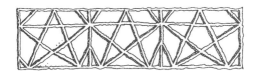

From old Buff Bill's Grave
and Museum with Tom
To the United States Mint where
coined money comes from,

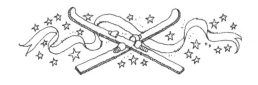

They zoomed through a tunnel—
the Moffat, that is.
Tom yelled, "Santa, you handle
this sleigh like a whiz!"

"You think that was swift, Tom,
grab hold of these ropes
'Cause now you will see
how I eat up the slopes!"

With a snap of his fingers
and wink of his eye,
Santa guided those reindeer
way up to the sky.

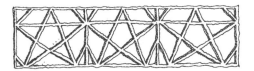

They made a great loop,
turned completely around,
Then, rushing like wild things,
dove straight for the ground.

St. Nick gave a warning,
"Watch out, Aspen and Vail!"
And hard to imagine,
his reindeer turned pale.

"Whoa," Santa yelled
as they tried to get stable,
But the sleigh got hung up,
jamming tight to a cable.

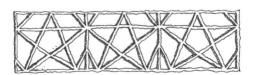

Dasher and Dancer,
suspended up high,
Looked at Tom, their eyes pleading,
"Please help us," they cried!

Prancer and Vixen
were poised upside down
With hooves in the air,
on their faces a frown.

Comet and Cupid,
their eyes buggin' wide,
Had changed places with Santa
and were seated inside!

But Donner and Blitzen,
screeching loudest of all,
Were totally convinced
they were going to fall!

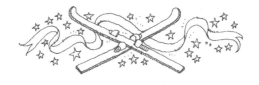

They jerked and they tugged,
thinking soon they would die,
Because in their panic
they forgot they could fly!

But Tommy was laughing
so hard, most hysterical,
He got everyone upright,
yelling, "Nick, it's a miracle!

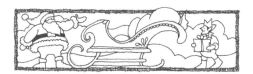

"This is the best time
that I've ever had.
I know why this season
makes everyone glad!"

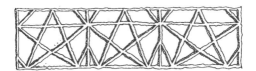

This hilarious affair,
caught by KFEL TV,
Made all want to perch
atop Santa's strong knee

To thank him and his deer
for the fabulous show
Performed for the people
of Colorado!

It was soon time to leave when
Nick thought he might lose it
While hearing the strains
of John Denver's sweet music:

"Rocky Mountain high," sang
the quartets of voices he heard.
From Durango to Boulder,
folks echoed the words.

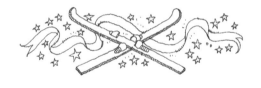

"To everyone here in
the Centennial State,
I must say goodnight,"
Nick cried. "It's quite late."

With a grin on Tom's face,
they all took their flight,
"Merry Christmas, Colorado,
to you all a Good Night!"